Self-Titled

Self-Titled

Geoffrey Brown

Coach House Books

Canada Council Conseil des Arts
for the Arts du Canada ONTARIO ARTS COUNCIL
CONSEIL DES ARTS DE L'ONTARIO Canadä

Published with the assistance of the Canada Council
for the Arts and the Ontario Arts Council. The
publisher also acknowledges the assistance of the
Government of Canada through the Book Publishing
Industry Development Program and the Government
of Ontario through the Ontario Book Publishing Tax
Credit Program.

LIBRARY AND ARCHIVES CANADA
CATALOGUING IN PUBLICATION

Brown, Geoffrey, 1965-
      Self-titled / Geoffrey Brown.

ISBN 1-55245-144-5

      I. Title.

PS8553.R68499S44 2004   C813´.5   C2004-904602-0

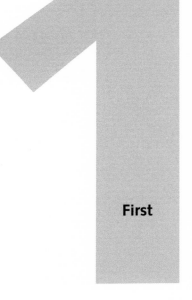

First

I behaved badly. I know I behaved badly. I am well aware that I behaved quite badly. I can offer no excuse. I know I should know better. I know. I know.

It was a mistake. I should have known it was a mistake. I should have known it would be a mistake. It was a mistake not to know it would be a mistake. I never should have not known it would be a mistake. It was a mistake to not know the mistake it would be.

We met. We arranged to meet. We met. We met at the place where we said we would meet. We arranged to meet at the place where we said we would meet at the time that we said we would meet at the place where we met. We met at the place where we said we would meet at the time that we said we would meet.

I gave myself an hour. I thought, An hour will be plenty. How long is an hour? How much can an hour take?

There was talk. There were things that were talked about. There were things that were talked about by me. I was not the only one who talked about the things that were talked about by me. Other people talked about the things that were talked about by me. There were others there who talked about the things that were talked about by me. I was not the only one who talked.

One morning, there she was. I saw her as I left. There she was. I left.

I was going to do it once. I wasn't going to do it once.

I never thought I would do what I did. I wondered what it would be like to do what I never thought I would do that I did. I wondered what it would be like after I did what I wondered what it would be like to do that I never thought I would do that I did.

It took an hour.

Don't do it, I thought. I said it to myself: Don't do it. I said it out loud. 'Don't do it.'

I could do anything. Whatever I wanted. Whatever there was.

I was supposed to wait. I made a deal. 'I'll wait. I'll wait a week.' I made another deal. I couldn't wait a week.

I kept thinking, What will happen? I kept thinking, What will happen if it happens?

I had never done it. I didn't know why I was doing it. I couldn't imagine why I was doing it.

She came over. It was the first time she came over. She came over for the first time and looked around. I let her look around. She moved about the room and looked around.

It happened often. Not all that often. But fairly often. You could say it happened fairly often. You could almost say it happened fairly often. It often happened fairly. You could almost say it happened fairly often, but you couldn't say it happened fairly. I don't think you could say it happened fairly. I don't think you should say it happened fairly. I don't think you should say it happened. I think it happened. But I don't think you should say it happened.

I kept changing. I couldn't decide. I changed. I decided. I couldn't decide.

She called me. She told me she was ready.

'I'm ready,' she said.

I told her I was ready. I told her I would pick her up. I went to pick her up. I picked her up.

I had a plan. I thought I had a plan. I thought I had a plan worked out. I thought I knew the plan I had. I thought I knew the plan I had that I was going to do.

I had only one. I only had one. I had one only. Only I had one.

I kept trying. I had no idea why I kept trying. I could never do what I kept trying to do. I had never done what I kept trying to do. I kept trying to do what I had never done. Trying to do what I had never done kept me trying.

This can't be done, I thought. I shouldn't be doing this. I shouldn't do this. I can't do this.

She told me what to do. She drew a diagram. She showed me. 'I understand,' I said.

I did it one way and then I did it a second way. I put it back the way it was before I did it the first way. I did it a third way. I tried to put it back the way it was the time I did it the second way. I couldn't remember how I did it when I did it the second way.

She said, 'I want to show you something. Come here.'

Inside it was dark. We felt our way.

'Slow down,' she said.

I stopped.

'What's wrong?'

'Don't stop.'

I moved.

'Come on.'

We went. The two of us. We went ahead. We met the others. There were others who were waiting who were there whom we were meeting. There were others who were waiting. They were waiting.

I decided to go. I could have stayed. I could have decided to stay. I could have decided to go. I could have decided. I wasn't being forced. No one said I had to go. No one said, 'Go.'

I turned around.

I heard my name. I turned around.

Someone waved. I couldn't make them out. They waved. I waved back.

I was doing it incorrectly. I was doing it wrong. Not the way it said. Not according. I was holding it wrong. I wasn't clutching. I had it wrong.

I liked the way she looked. She said she liked to look. She said she liked to watch. I let her watch. I let her watch a lot. She never asked to touch. She never tried to touch. She only ever looked. I think she liked to look. I think she liked to watch.

I went first.

'Your turn,' I said.

'No. Your turn.'

I went.

'Your turn,' I said.

No one paid attention. Not to me. No one paid attention to me. They paid me no attention.

I promised I would go. I went. I promised I would go. I went. There was no one there. I promised I would go. I went. There was no one there. I promised I would go. I didn't want to go.

I got it done. I got one done. I still had two to do. No, that's not right. I had as many to do as I hadn't done. Of those I had done, there were none I hadn't done. Of those I hadn't done, I had as many yet to do.

I went back many times. I don't know how many times I went back. I can't remember how many times I went back. I remember going back many times. Numerous times. I went back. I went back. I went back. I went back. More times than that.

'Listen,' she said.

'Look,' she said.

'Are you ready?' she said.

'Do you want to?' she said.

I took what I had and went over. I didn't have much. It fit in a bag. It fit in one bag. What it was was what fit in a bag. A bag was all it was. The size of the bag. The it it was was not without the bag. Without the bag the it it was was not.

I went first. She went second. I went first. She went second. We went one after the other. Me first, her second. First one, then the other. Me, then her.

I wanted to go. I was ready to go. I thought I was ready to go. I felt I was ready to go. I think I was ready to go. I think I thought I was ready to go.

She told me she didn't care. I knew for a fact she cared. She cared.

'I know you care.'

'I don't care,' she said.

'You care.'

She cared.

It was easier than I thought. I thought it would be hard. It was hard.

I moved back. I went forward. I stepped back. Stepped forward. It was not a hesitation. I wouldn't say I hesitated. I wouldn't say the stepping back and forth was a hesitation. I wouldn't hesitate to say the stepping back and forth was not a hesitation.

I liked to think that I was prepared. If being prepared was possible. If being prepared was something for which one could be prepared. I liked to think that I was preparing to prepare.

She held up her hand. 'Did you hear that?'

'Wait,' she said. 'Stop,' she said. 'Listen,' she said.

I waited. I stopped. I listened.

She was in the room next door. She'd gone into the room next door. She hadn't come out of the room next door. She was in the room next door alone. She was in the room next door with no one who would make her in a room with someone who would make her not alone. The room next door was not alone.

Sometimes someone knocked. Sometimes someone who knocked knocked at night. Sometimes when someone who knocked knocked at night I was in bed. Not always. Not always when someone who knocked knocked at night was I in bed. But sometimes when someone who knocked knocked at night I was in bed.

I could hear her talking. I could hear her voice. I could hear the murmur of her voice. I couldn't hear her talking. I could hear her voice. I could hear the murmur of her voice.

I had no plan.

I had no nothing.

I thought something good would happen. I kept thinking something good would happen. I thought something would happen that was good. I kept thinking something would happen that was good. It was good that I kept thinking. That was good.

It took a long time. It was taking a long time. It was taking longer. It was longer. It was long. This long. It was this long. It was taking this long. As long as this.

The first time was difficult. The second time was difficult. The third time was difficult. The fourth time was difficult.

I didn't know what I was getting. I was getting something. When I saw what I was getting I would know what I was getting. I would see what I was getting. I would know what I was getting. I was getting something I would know.

I didn't use it often. I didn't use what I didn't use as often as I thought I would use it. I thought I would use it often. I thought I would use what I didn't use more often.

There was silence. There was no noise. There was a noise. I went to the window. It was dark. I looked into the night. It was dark and there was a noise and it was night.

I was never going to tell. I told myself, 'I'll never tell.' I had no reason not to tell. There was no reason not to tell. No reason. I had no reason.

I felt nothing. That space. Where there might have been remorse. There was nothing. I felt nothing. The space of nothing.

No one ever talked about it. No one wanted to talk about it. No one ever mentioned it. It was never spoken of. No one ever spoke of it.

I'd heard everything there was to hear. I heard another thing there was to hear. I'd heard everything there was to hear once I'd heard another thing there was to hear.

I didn't know how they could do it. How could they do it? Over and over, again and again. They could keep doing it and doing it. I didn't know how they could do it. They didn't ever stop doing it. Did they ever stop doing it? I didn't think they ever stopped doing it. Ever. Ever think they didn't. Didn't ever think. Didn't. Ever.

There was no call. There was not a call. There never was a call that was the call that never was.

It didn't bother me. It never bothered me.

I did the same thing every day. I did the same thing every day. The same thing. Every day. Every day.

I told myself not to worry. I told myself to never worry. Things would be all right. Things would all work out. Nothing's going to happen, I thought. Nothing will go wrong.

She was out there. Looking. I went out. I stayed behind. Followed. Pretended I was looking. She was looking. She looked.

Now what happens? I thought. I let the day go by. I did nothing all day but decide. I decided. I was not prepared. I got ready to prepare. I decided to get ready to prepare. I happened to get ready to prepare. I prepared to get ready to happen.

I thought she might be coming back. I couldn't tell. It looked as though she might be coming back. It was hard to tell. She might be coming back, I thought. She wasn't supposed to be coming back. I was looking. Watching. Checking.

'She might be coming back,' I said.

No response. There was no response. No one was responding. No one had response.

It wasn't right. I knew it wasn't right. I knew full well it wasn't right. It was all right, though. It was all right if it wasn't right. Right?

I turned it around. I turned it around. I turned it around. I turned it around.

It was in her mouth. She put it in her mouth. She took it out of her mouth.

'That's enough of that.'

I wondered if she knew. She didn't know. Sometimes I wondered if she knew. She didn't know. I thought she knew. She didn't know. I was sure she knew. I was almost sure she knew. She didn't know.

Nothing worked. Everything was wrong. I did what I could. Everything was wrong. Nothing worked.

'Now,' she said. 'Begin.'

She didn't make a sound. She didn't say a word.

I was almost done.

'Begin again,' she said.

They were open. She opened them. Spread them. Put them together. Pulled them apart. Together. Apart.

I tried to put it in. I tried to find a place to put it in. I wanted to find a place to put it in. I wanted just to put it in. I thought that I could put it in. If I could find a place to put it in.

'Hold it there,' she said.

I held it there.

'Don't move,' she said.

I didn't move.

'Now move,' she said. 'Slowly. Back and forth.'

I moved slowly. Back and forth.

'Not so fast,' she said. 'Slow it down,' she said.

I moved it slowly. Back and forth. I moved it up and down.

'Don't,' she said.

She was on her back. Her hips in the air. She thrust them up. Brought them down. Her arms by her side. Palms flat on the floor. She raised her hips.

Brought them down. She used her palms to brace herself. She raised her hips. She brought them down. She pressed her palms against the floor.

It came out. I took a towel. I wiped it off. I dried it. I put the towel back.

I couldn't swallow. It hurt to swallow. I had to swallow. It hurt to swallow. I couldn't swallow. I swallowed.

It was a simple matter. Cut.

The house was dark.
        'Unlock the door.'
        We went inside. Turned on the lights.

I dialed six-nine. No one answered. I dialed six-nine. No one answered. I dialed six-nine. No one answered. For several days no one answered. Then someone answered.

It was open so I opened it. I looked at what was there where I had opened it. I looked where it was opened. I didn't pick it up from where I'd opened it. I didn't take it out from where I'd opened it. I didn't even touch it, really. All I did was open it and look at what I'd seen before I'd opened it but now saw where I'd opened it. It wasn't it, but open that I saw.

She handed me money. 'Count it.'
    I counted it.
    'Count it again.'
    I counted it again.
    'How much is there?'
    I counted it again.

They were somewhere. They existed somewhere. Somewhere they existed. Somewhere they existed. They existed somewhere. Somewhere they were.

There were two. She had them both.
    'One goes here and one goes here.'
    I watched. She showed me where to put my hands.
    'When I say push, you push.'

She took a breath.
'Push.'

She got caught. Called. Told me where she was. I got dressed. Got her. Brought her back. Cleaned her up.

'You can spend the night,' I said.
'No,' she said. 'I can't.'

I couldn't sit still. I got up. I stood up. Walked. Came back. Sat. Stood. Went. Peed.

She wasn't around. She didn't show up. I waited. I left a note. 'Take the high road,' it said.

I told her not to worry. She worried.
'Don't worry.'
She worried.
'I worry.'

It wasn't working. It wasn't working out. I had no idea what it was that wasn't working out. Whatever it was, it wasn't working out.

No one wanted it. I offered it around. People looked at it. I let people look at it. I let people take it home. 'Live with it,' I said.

I was almost caught. I was never caught. I was sure that I was caught. I was sure that I was almost caught. I was never caught. I was almost caught.

I pushed her out of the way. She was in the way. I pushed her out of the way.

I was upset. I got upset. I wasn't upset. I didn't get upset.

I thought, If I have to, I will. I don't want to, but I will. I think if I have to, I will. I think I will if I have to. I will think if I have to. I have to think if I will. If I will I think I have to. I doubt I will if I have to. I will have to doubt if I will.

'I can't wear this,' she said. 'I'll hurt myself.'
    'No, you won't,' I said.
    'It looks a little dangerous,' she said.

'It is a little dangerous.'

She put it on.

She took it off.

'Put it on,' I said.

I landed on my stomach. My forehead hit the ground. There were people there. 'Are you all right?'

I tried to stand.

'That was something.'

I checked for blood. My shirt was wet. I wiped my brow.

'Do that again.'

I lay back down.

What was I supposed to do? How long did I have to wait?

I did one. I did one one day. I did one one day, got it done, did another. I could have done another one another day. I could have done another one another day and another one another day after that.

She was on her way. She was on her way. I had to get things ready. She was on her way. I had to get things ready. It should have all been done. It should have been all done.

I tried not to notice. I pretended not to notice. I closed my eyes and didn't notice. I knew what I wasn't noticing. I could hear what I wasn't noticing. I could hear things break. I could hear things rip. I closed my eyes and not noticed. Things broke. Things ripped. I failed to notice.

I put it in a couple times. I stuck it in a couple spots. I took it out.

I pushed her down. I pushed her down. 'Get up.' She got up. I pushed her down. 'Get up.' I pushed. She stepped back. Turned. Ran.

She knocked on my door. I let her in. Offered her coffee. Took her out. Showed her the grounds. 'These are the grounds,' I said. I waved my hands. Brought her in. We went through the house. She let herself out. I rinsed the cups.

I bought an address book. Or, I don't know, a notepad, say. I put it by the phone.

'You're angry,' she said.

I looked up from my book.

'I can tell you're angry. Why are you so angry?'

I set my book down.

I had other things to do. I had other things I had to do. Things other than the things that were things I had to do. There was nothing I could do.

She tried to get up. I yelled. How many times? I kicked. Missed.

I pulled it out. I thought it might make a noise. I thought it might pop. I thought it might make a popping noise. I wanted to hear it pop. I wanted it to pop. I pulled it out so I could hear it pop.

She was there. I called. I called her twice. I called again.

I didn't mean to. I didn't. I didn't mean to do what I did without meaning to do it. I didn't mean to go so far as to do what I didn't mean to do. I don't know why I didn't stop from doing what I didn't mean to do. I didn't want to stop.

I moved them back and forth. I moved one back and forth. I moved the other back and forth. I pushed them back and forth. I pushed them forward. Pulled them back. I picked them up. Put them down. Moved them back. Forth.

She came. She looked. She came, looked, left. Sometimes she came, looked, left, came back.

I stuck a finger in her mouth. 'Suck.' I pulled it out and pushed it in. She gagged.

My arm was sore. I couldn't keep my arm still. It hurt to keep it still. I moved it. I swung it back. I lifted it. It hurt to move.

She heard it. She said she heard it. 'I heard it,' she said. 'Did you hear it?'

'What?'

'What I heard.'

'I heard something.'

'Was what you heard what I heard?'

'I heard what I heard.'

I could have put more in. I could have put in more.

I was going to try again. I was going to try once more. I tried again. I tried once more. I was going to try again. I was going to try once more.

I had to take it out. It was trouble. What it was I had to take out was trouble. What it was I had to take out I had to take out because what it was was causing trouble. I had to take out what it was that was causing trouble. I had to take it out, I thought.

I looked. 'It won't go in,' I said.

I stuck it in.

I wasn't going to do any more. I was going to do one more. I wasn't going to do one more. I wasn't going to do any more.

I had some on. I put some on. I already had some on.

She left. She arrived. She left. She came back. She went back. She came back. She went back. She came out. She went in.

I had her from behind, arms around her waist. She fell forward, almost down. I pulled back. Heaved her up. Her arms limp. Swung. The sun came up.

She pointed at the door. 'In there,' she said.
    I went in.
    She shut the door.

'Don't touch it,' she said. When I didn't touch it, she said, 'Go ahead. Touch it.'
    I touched it.

'How did it feel?'

'I don't know.'

'You can touch it again,' she said. 'Touch it again.'

I went ahead. Pushed through. Used my arms. Used my hands. Squeezed past. Got through. Went on.

Something happened. It felt good.

I stayed in my seat. I didn't get up. I sat. I sat up. I sat down. I never got up.

Every afternoon I took a walk. I walked.

I waited. It was late. It was too late. She wouldn't come. I waited.

I helped her dress. Picked out her clothes. 'Put this on.' I zipped her. Buttoned her. Smoothed her out.

I got to thinking I was wrong. I got to thinking I was right. Maybe I was right, I thought. Maybe I was right all along. Maybe I only thought I was wrong, but all along I was wrong about not being right. Maybe I was not right about being wrong. Maybe being right was not right. Maybe all along being wrong was right.

I opened it. She told me I could open it. 'Go ahead and open it,' she said.

One night I thought of something we could do.

'That's not something I want to do,' she said.

I went away and thought. I thought of something we could do which was not what I thought we could do before.

'That's not something I want to do either,' she said.

I couldn't believe what happened happened. I didn't believe what happened would happen. I couldn't believe what I didn't believe would happen happened. I knew that what I didn't believe would happen would happen. I wanted what I didn't believe would happen to happen.

I was hoping that what I didn't believe would happen would happen. I couldn't believe what I didn't believe would happen happened.

I sat down. I was tired. I got into bed. Closed my eyes. I didn't sleep. I felt as though I slept. I didn't sleep. I might have slept.

She put her hand on my head. She let it rest a moment there.

It came and it went. It came and went. It came and went. It will come. It will go. It will come and go. It will come and it will go.

I watched what she could do. She said, 'Watch what I can do.' I watched.

I felt like grabbing her. I felt like grabbing on to her. I felt like reaching up and grabbing on to her.

I fell asleep on the sofa. When I woke up, the room was dark, the TV was off. I checked the clock.

'Stick your fist in here,' she said.

I tried. I stuck my fingers in. I stuck in two, then three, then four.

'See if you can make a fist,' she said.

I moved my fingers. I tried to make a fist. I pulled my fingers out. Made a fist.

'This can't fit,' I said.

'Try,' she said.

I tried. I made a fist. I tried to put it in.

I stayed in bed until she left. I listened. She locked the door. It clicked. I heard it click. I heard her going down the stairs.

I opened it. I slit it. Sliced it. Peeled back what I'd opened. Pried. Pulled. Closed what I'd pried.

I decided I would bring it home. I wasn't sure I wanted it, but I thought, Bring it home. Bring it home and then decide. I got it home. I decided. I didn't know what to do.

I could hear them. I could hear them slow. I could hear they didn't stop. I could hear them disappear. I could hear them slow, not stop, then disappear.

There were things I didn't like. The things I didn't like I did what I could to fix. I tried my best to fix the things I didn't like. I changed the order of the things I didn't like. I took things out I didn't like in. I left some in I did like in. Left some in I didn't like in. I left things in that I didn't like in. Left some in I didn't like in along with the things I did like in. No one would notice.

Maybe they wanted them. Maybe not. If they didn't, okay. If they didn't want them, okay. That was okay. If they didn't want them, that was okay. If the ones that didn't want them didn't want them, okay.

It was the last time. It wasn't the last time. It was always the last time. It was never the last time. I said it was the last time. I thought it was the last time. This is the last time, I thought. 'This time is the last time,' I said.

She kept them. She wouldn't give them back. I asked her if she would give them back. 'No,' she said. 'They're mine,' she said. I asked her for them back.

Maybe it was me. Maybe I was to blame. Maybe it was my fault. Maybe I was the one.

It looked better than it was. It wasn't as good as it looked. In my opinion, that which looked better than it was wasn't as good as it looked. That which looked better than it was wasn't even close to being as good as it looked. That which looked better than it was looked terrific. I thought it looked terrific. But that which looked better than it was was not that good. That which wasn't as good as it looked wasn't very good. It wasn't that good.

I didn't know what would happen next. I never knew what would happen next.

'Don't come back,' she said. 'Do not come back.'

I didn't take it. I should have taken it. I should have taken what I didn't take when I should have taken it. I didn't take what I didn't take. I didn't think I wanted what I didn't take when I should have taken it. I didn't think I wanted what I didn't take the chance to take when I should have taken it. I don't know how I got what I didn't take. I borrowed what I got that I don't know how I got that I didn't take. Or I stole what I got that I don't know how I got that I didn't take. Or maybe I took what got that I thought I didn't take that I don't know how I got. I should have taken it.

I kept recipes. I clipped recipes. I clipped them out of magazines. Newspapers. I kept them in the kitchen. In a file.

There was nothing to eat. There was nothing in the house. Nothing. There might have been some nuts. There might have been some peanuts. There was an apple. There was one apple. I ate that.

I asked for something stark. It was pretty stark. The thing that I asked for to be something stark was something pretty stark. I think the whole of the thing that I asked for to be something stark was something pretty stark.

I copied it. I wrote down what was copied. I used a pencil to write down what was copied. I typed what I used a pencil to write down what it was that was what I copied. I printed what it was that was typed that I copied that was pencil. I taped what I copied what I wrote what I pencilled what I printed to the wall. I said to myself what I'd taped what I'd typed what I'd copied what I'd printed to the wall. Recited what I'd taped what I'd copied what I'd said to the wall. I said it to myself.

I didn't stop. I never stopped. I said I'd stop. I said I stopped. I didn't stop. I never stopped.

I was getting rid of things. Piece by piece and very slowly, I was getting rid of things. I was throwing away the things I was getting rid of. The things I was getting rid of, I was throwing them away.

I could never remember where I wrote things. Grocery lists, messages, addresses, phone numbers. I never knew. I wrote them down on anything.

I took a walk. I got up, got dressed and took a walk. Put on my scarf. My gloves. Went outside. Walked.

I couldn't get in. She wouldn't let me in. I'd been in before. She'd let me in before. This time she wouldn't let me in.

I went to bed. I'd only just got up. I went back. I showered. I shaved. I brushed. I drank. I made a sandwich. I went out. I got the mail. Came back. Did dishes. Washed dishes. Dried dishes. Put dishes away. I went upstairs. I went to bed.

She was expecting me. She knew I was coming. Maybe she knew I was coming. She knew. She knew I was coming.

I decided to stay. I decided to stay a little longer. A little longer. A little while longer.

She whispered. I had trouble hearing her. 'Please speak up,' I said. I had trouble hearing her. She whispered.

I heard her land. I went to pick her up. She was still asleep. I bent down. Lifted her. Set her on the bed. I set her near the wall. Left the room. Closed the door. I heard her land.

I followed her. I watched her. I watched her walk inside. I watched her close the door. I stood across the street. The days were getting short.

It was she. I was sure it was she. I called her name. People turned. Other people turned. She was moving fast. I called her name. No one turned. Moving fast. I called her name.

Maybe I was wrong. It could be I was wrong. I might not have been wrong.

There was still the other one. The other one might pop, I thought.

I never paid. I promised I would pay. I wrote the cheque. I think I wrote the cheque. I put the cheque in an envelope. I never sent it.

I came awake. I remembered. Right away. I remembered. Maybe I was wrong. Maybe it's not true, I thought. I closed my eyes. Tried to think.

I was going to make a list. I should have thought of that before. I would make a list. Of course. A list.

It was lost. Maybe it was lost. It may be it was lost. It was lost. I wasn't getting it back. It certainly seemed to be lost. It certainly seemed it was lost.

'Do you want one?' she said. 'I have another one.'
    'How many do you have?'
    'I have this one and another one. You can have it. Here. Take it.'

I took it.

'I have another one.'

I sent them again. The same ones. I sent them again. I'd already sent them. I sent them again.

I was leaving. I was leaving early. I might have been leaving early. I might not have been leaving early. I wasn't leaving early. I was staying.

I got up late. It was after ten. I got up. Brushed my teeth. Took a shower. Went downstairs. I made some tea. I boiled an egg. A hard-boiled egg.

All of it was gone. All of it was gone. Most of it was gone.

I was going to have to go soon. I hadn't gone yet, but soon I would. Soon I would go. I was going soon.

I figured it out. Did the calculations. I knew the score.

We agreed to meet. We thought we should meet. 'We should meet,' we said. She picked a place. I told her I would be there. 'I'll be there,' I said.

It should have been gone. I should have been gone.

Someone knocked. They knocked. I heard them cough.

'Go ahead and touch it,' she said. She held it out.

I didn't want to touch it. I touched it. I pulled my hand away.

'Feel better now?'

I held my hand away.

I took some out. I took some out. I put some in. I put others in. Others I took out. Some of those I took out, I put back in. I didn't put them all back in. I didn't know what I'd taken out and put back in from what I'd put in and never taken out.

It went well. I thought it went well. I didn't feel as though it wouldn't go well. I felt as though it would go well. I thought it went well. It went well.

I pounded on the door. I used my palm. I made a fist. I hit the door. I made a fist. I hit the door. I hit the door. I hit the door. How many times can you hit a door?

She put it in her mouth. She put it in a bit. She put it in more. She put it in some more. Some more of it put in.

I was there more often. I was there more and more often. I was there where before I wasn't there. When in the past I was not there, now I was there.

I'd thrown away a lot. I'd thrown away many. I didn't like to think about how many I'd thrown away. How many had I thrown away?

Was I thirty-five years old?

I set aside my book. I stood up and stretched. I touched my toes. I touched the floor. Gripped my ankles. Breathed in. Breathed out. Counted. To eleven. Sat down. Picked up my book.

I squatted. I actually squatted. I squatted down and stood up. I did it again. I did it again. I did it every morning. Ten times. I did it at night. Or in the morning. Or after lunch.

I thought something was going to happen. I thought something was going to happen soon. Something's going to happen, I thought. Something's going to happen soon.

I watched. She disappeared. I thought she might come back. She might come back, I thought.

I made a request. I made a simple request. An outrageous request. Simple. It was a simple request.

Things came back. Some things came back in several days. Other things took a month or two.

I had it taken off. The place was empty. I took a form. I filled it out. I had it taken off.

I sent her a small collection. She returned it. 'No,' she said. I repackaged it. It was the same collection, repackaged. It might have been the packaging.

I put it on and pushed it in. Leave it there awhile, I thought. Leave it overnight. I took it out.

Did it matter? Did it matter? Did it?

I offered to reheat her dinner.
        'I'm not hungry,' she said.

I was going to send her something. I didn't know what I was going to send her. I was going to send her something that was something that I didn't know what it was. That was exactly what I was going to send her. It didn't matter what it was I sent her except that what it was I sent her had to be something that I didn't know what it was. It had to be something that I didn't know what it was. I could have sent her something. I wanted to send her something.

I was not going. Now I was not going. I was not going now. I was now not going. I now was not going. Was I not going now?

She didn't know she had it. I didn't think she knew she had it. I didn't see how she would miss it if it were gone. How would she miss it if it were gone? She wouldn't miss it if it were gone. She wouldn't even know it was gone. She didn't even know she had it. I didn't think she even knew she had it. It wouldn't be stealing. It wasn't as though I would be stealing.

I didn't manage to get it right. I did try to get it right. I did try to get it right. I didn't manage to get it right. I intended to get it right. I intended to get it right.

It was late. Time was up. I wasn't done. I had to go. I had to leave. I packed. I put away my things. Folded this. Stacked that. Ate the last of something.

I turned on the light. It was light. I turned on the light.

I thought I maybe noticed. I thought I might have noticed. I took another look. I couldn't tell. I stood still. I looked. Even if I had. Even if I had noticed. I hadn't. I hadn't noticed.

I wondered if she'd sent it. She told me she would send it. I wondered if she'd sent it.

I wasn't using names. I wasn't naming names. It didn't matter to me. Names.

It was the only thing I ever thought about. It wasn't the only thing I ever thought about. I did think about it. I had thought about it. It was something I had thought about. I thought about it.

I didn't know what I should say. I didn't know if I should say anything. I could have said something. I could have come right out and said something. But what would I have said? I know what I'd have said. I'd said what I'd have said. I'd already said.

I made a list. I wrote things down. Made a list. I had a list. I made a list.

I stopped. Listened. There was no one. There was nothing.

I managed to stop it. It took some time. For a long time I couldn't stop it.

I ate every now and then. An apple in the morning. A sandwich or some soup for lunch.

I was waiting for someone to see. Not just anyone. Someone not the one that wasn't one that was the one.

They slid right out. I slid them right out. They slid right out.

I wanted something more. I thought I wanted something more.

It was there when I arrived. It wasn't there when I was leaving. I think it was there when I arrived.

I knew what happened. I knew full well what happened. I full well knew what happened.

I couldn't remember. I could barely remember. I wasn't sure I could barely remember. I didn't know that I couldn't remember. I didn't know what I could barely remember.

I was wrong. It turned out I was wrong. As it happened, I was wrong. I wasn't right. It wasn't true. It was not true. It was not the truth. It wasn't the truth. It wasn't true. I wasn't right. I was wrong. As it happened, I was wrong. It turned out I was wrong.

There was no reason to continue. I couldn't think of a reason to continue. I did try to think of a reason to continue. I tried to think of two or three reasons to continue.

She said, 'Listen to me.'
    She said, 'Are you listening to me?'
    She said, 'Listen to me.'
    'I want you to listen to me,' she said.
    'I want you to listen,' she said.
    'You listen,' she said. 'To me.'

I lied. Everything I told was a lie. It was all a lie. None of what I told was anything but what was not the truth. All was not the truth of what I told. It was not the truth.

No one ever knew. It is over now. No one knows.

It took about a week. No, it didn't. It took a little longer than a week. If I said it took about a week, I guess I meant it took a little longer than a week.

I was almost finished. I had almost finished. For the second time, I had almost finished. I was finished all I had to finish to be where being finished was all but finished.

I didn't feel bad. I should have felt bad. I probably should have felt bad. I didn't feel bad. What does it mean to feel bad? I wondered. What does it mean to be someone who doesn't feel bad? What does it mean to fail to feel bad? What does it mean to fail?

I did some rearranging. I moved some things around. I seemed to have more places where things were not. I moved some things to places where things were not. I seemed to have more places where things were not.

I still had the things I never threw out. I never threw out the things I still had. I had out the things I never threw. Still.

I wasn't sure how clear I was. I didn't know how clear I was. I didn't know if what I hadn't said had left what I had said much clearer. It was clear I hadn't said what was left to say. What was left to say I hadn't said.

I could still feel myself. I could feel myself inside. I still could feel myself inside. Inside I still could feel. Inside myself I still.

I had the address on my desk. I had the address on my desk for weeks. I had the address on my desk for months. I wrote the address down and put it on my desk. I left the address on my desk. I saw the address every morning. On my desk. Every morning.

There wasn't much left. There was a little left. Not that much. Not enough to matter.

It was warm inside. It felt like nothing else. It felt like something new. It felt like something warm.

I had a quiet afternoon. Wrote a letter. Read the paper. Drank a beer. Ate a salad.

Second

I'll be honest with you. Can I be honest with you? Let me be honest with you. There was another. There was another other. There was another other nother. No, there was not. There was no other. There was no another. There was not another. There was never there another. Never not another. There was only one. There was only me. It was only me. I was only me. I was me. Begin again. It was me. It was just me. I was alone. There was just me. Alone. Me. I was me. I was just. The me that was I was just. The me that was just was just me. The me that was just I. The me was just just. Just the just. The me that was I.

I was the me. I was the me that was just. I was just the me that was the I. I was just I. I was I. I was just. I've lied. I've already lied. Already I've lied. I've lied already. Listen. Are you listening? Listen. The nights were long. The nights were all long. All the nights were long. All the days were long. All the nights and all the days were long. The nights and days were always long. The nights and days were almost always long. The nights and days were almost always all long. The nights and days were almost always nights and days. I am having trouble. I am going to be having trouble. I will be having trouble. I have been having trouble. I have had trouble. I have been trouble. Have I been trouble? Have I had trouble? Am I having trouble? Am I trouble? I should say 'I.' I meant to say 'I.' I think I did say 'I.' Did I say 'I'? There must be another way. There has to be another way. There is another way. There is always another way. There is always another day. Another long day. Another fucking day. I didn't do anything. I couldn't do anything. What could I do? There wasn't anything I could do. Fucking days. Fucking nights. Fucking long nights. Anything I couldn't do I didn't do. Anything I didn't do I couldn't do. I couldn't do what I didn't do. I couldn't not do what I didn't do. I couldn't not do anything. I couldn't do anything I didn't do. What could I do that I didn't do? What didn't I do that I could do? Did I do anything? What did I do? What didn't I do? I didn't do what I couldn't do. Anything I couldn't not do I didn't not do. Did I? Did I? Fuck. Days. I couldn't not do anything? Anything I not could do I do not could? Do you want me to tell you something? Do you? Do you want me? Let me tell you something. Let me tell you something else. It happened like this. It could have happened like this. It could have happened just like this. It could have happened just like this the way I said it happened just like this. Just the way I said it happened. The way it just happened. I was all alone. I wasn't all alone. I was not alone. I was not at all. I was not. I am not. I am not at all. I keep to myself. I kept to myself. There was no one. No one was there. There was no one there. There was one there. There was only one there. Only one was there. Was only one there? Was only one was there? Was there only one was? Was there only one was there? What was was there? What was was that that was there? Do you know what was was there? Do you know what there was there? Do you know what this is? Do you want to know what this is? Do you want me to tell you what this is? Do you? Want it! Want it! I went. I went over. Over I went. Sometimes I went over. It wasn't a relief. There was no relief. There might have been relief. I might have felt relief. It was brief. If I felt relief it was brief. It was brief relief. If I felt relief the relief I felt was brief relief. This is my belief. It is my belief the relief I felt was brief relief. Brief relief. I give up. No, I don't. I don't give up. I won't give up. I will not give up. I will not give up now. Now I will not give up. No longer will I give up. I can't keep track. I cannot keep track. I can never keep track. I cannot ever keep track. How can I ever keep track? How can I ever forever keep track? How ever forever? Forever however? However I track I can never forever. There are too many. There are too many to track. There is too much to track. Too many, too much. Too many such. Too much such. I clutch at such. I am not what I was. I am not what I was not at all. Today I read. I read today. Today I read all day today. Today all day today I read. I read what I read all day today. All today I read what I read. You heard me. I said I read. I read in bed. I said I read in bed. I said I read all day today. In bed all day today I read. I said. It doesn't make a difference. Does it? Does it make a difference? What difference does it make? Does it make any difference? Does it make any actual difference? Does the difference it makes actually make any difference? Does the actual difference it makes actually make any difference at all? Do I make a difference? Do I make any difference? I could do anything. Anything I could do would not make a difference. I could not make a difference at anything I do. Do I do anything that makes a difference? Do I? Do I do? She didn't come back. She never came back. I could do anything. I could do anything I wanted to do. Anything I wanted to do, I could do. I could do anything I wanted to do anytime I wanted to do anything. Anything I wanted to do would be anything I could do. Anything I wanted to do would never be anything I couldn't do. Anything I couldn't do that I wanted to do wasn't anything I wanted to do. There wasn't anything I wanted to do that wasn't anything I couldn't do. There was nothing. There was no one. No one was there. Nothing was there. No one and nothing was there. No one was there where nothing was there. There wasn't a thing. There wasn't one thing. There wasn't one single thing. There wasn't one single fucking thing. There wasn't one single fucking thing that wasn't a thing that was fucking. There was a thing. There was one thing. There was one fucking thing. There was one thing fucking. Slowly it started. It started slowly. She didn't come home. Sometimes she didn't come home. Sometimes when she said she was coming home she wasn't coming home. Where was she? Why won't she call? I want her to call.

Do you know why she won't call? Do you know what happened? Can you tell me what happened? Who can tell me what happened? I can tell me what happened. I tell me what happened every day. Every day I tell me what happened. Every day it happened. I tell me every day it happened and every day I tell me it happened. Let me tell you what happened. Finally. At last. Let me tell you. I will tell you. I will tell you what happened. I will tell you at last. Finally. Fuck you. Fuck you if I'm going to tell you. Fuck you if I'm going to tell you anything. I've lost interest. I'm losing interest. Fuck you. Interest is loss. My interesting loss. There should be something here. Here there should be something. Something here should be there. I saw it. I stole it. Right away I stole it. I stole it right away. I stole it away. I stole it right. I stole away. I stole away after I stole it away. I stole right away after I stole it right away. Right away I stole away after I stole it right away. Right after I stole it right, I stole right away. I stole right away after I stole it right. Right away I stole what I stole right away. Right. I write. I write away. Every day I write away. I write every day away. I keep asking what happened. Do you know what happened? Do you happen to know what happened? Do you? Do you know? Do you happen to know? I don't know. I know what I know. What I happen to know. I happen to know what I happen to know. I don't know what happened. There was nothing. Was there nothing? What was nothing? What was the nothing? Where was there nothing? What nothing was there? What was the nothing that was there? What nothing was there that was nothing there? Where was the nothing that was not there? Where was nothing there? Where was nothing? I paid no attention. No attention at all. No attention whatsoever. I paid no attention whatsoever. I never paid attention ever. I never ever paid attention whatsoever. I never whatsoever paid attention ever. Whatever I paid was never whatsoever attention ever. Never ever whatsoever. I kept going. I kept going where I was going. Where I was going was where I kept going. I kept going where I was going never knowing quite where I was going. Where I was going was never quite where I was going. Where was I going? Was I not where I was going? Was I not where I was getting? I wasn't getting to where I was going. I wasn't. Was not. Where I was getting was not where I was going to get. I was not getting to go where I was going to get. Where the fuck was I going? I was going fuck. Fuck going. Go fucking. Day after day. Night after night. Day after night after night after day. I can't remember. I can't remember last night. I can't remember today. I can't remember right now. Right now I can't remember today. Right now I can't remember last night or today or right now. I can't remember right now right now. I can't remember today what I remembered last night. Last night I remembered. I remembered what I remembered. I remembered last night. I took a bit away. I took a little bit away. I took a little bit of some away. I took a little bit of some of what I took away. Some of what I took away was some of the little bit I took. Some of the little bit I took away was a bit of the little bit of some of what I took away. I took away some. There won't be much. There might be much. Maybe there might be much. There might be maybe much. Maybe much might be. Much might be maybe. Maybe might is much. Maybe much is might. Might maybe be much. I should have last night. I could have last night. Last night I could have. Last night I should have. I should have taken away a bit of what I took away last night. Last night I could have taken away a bit of what I should have taken away. I could have bit the fucker. I should have bit the fucker. I should have the fucker bit. The bit I took away should have taken me away. Take me away. I should have a bit of the fucker bit off away. Do you think it should matter? Do you think it matters? Should it matter? Should you think it matters? Should you think? Do you think you should think it matters? Do you think you should think should it matter? Should it matter that you think? Think you I should bite the fucker? I've decided it is mine. I've decided that it's mine. I'm not sure that it is. I'm not sure it is that. I've decided that it is. I've decided it is that. I've decided that. This time there is less. This time I confess. I confess this time there is less. Less to confess. Confess there is less. More or less. More or less, this time there is less. There is less, more or less. There is more or less less. I feel better. I feel better more or less. More or less better. I feel better than I felt when I was more or less better than I feel now. It's the same. Isn't it the same? It is the same. It's not the same. What is same? Is change the same? What is change? Something's changed. I have changed. Something in me has changed. Is change not the same? It all is the same. Nothing has changed. I knew their names. I knew them by name. I knew some of them by name. Some of them I knew by several names. Some of them knew I knew some of them by several names. Some of them I knew by no name. They helped. I was angry. They tried to help. They always tried to help. They always tried to always help. They always tried to always help but I was always angry. I am still angry. I am always angry. I was angry before. I was angry before I was angry before. I was angry before I was angry and I was angry after I was angry. I was more angry before. I was more hungry before. I was angry, I was hungry, I was trying to keep track. More than before. I was more than before. I was more than I was before. Before I was nothing. Before I was more I was nothing before. I was nothing after. I was more. I was more before. I was so much more before. Wasn't that enough? That was enough, wasn't it? That was enough. Wasn't it? Wasn't enough enough? Enough was enough. Enough of that. Enough of that was enough. Enough was enough of that. I kept feeling more than enough. I kept feeling more better. I kept feeling more than enough better than enough. Enough was better. Better than enough. It was better than enough, wasn't it? Wasn't it better than enough to be enough? Wasn't enough enough? I was better than I was feeling. Was I enough? I wanted out. I wasn't in. I wanted out of what I wasn't in. What I wanted out of was what I wasn't in. I kept getting better. I kept getting coffee. I kept getting better coffee. I coughed. I got better. I got better at coughing. I got better at coffee. I saw what happened. I didn't see what happened. I didn't see what I saw. I didn't happen. I didn't happen to see what I saw. I didn't happen to see what happened. I didn't happen to see what

– 72 –

I saw happen. I said I saw what happened. I saw what I said. I said what I saw. I said what I saw I said. I saw what I said I saw. I saw what I saw I said. I saw what I said I said. I wasn't watching. I was refusing to watch. I watched what I was refusing. I refused what I was watching. Watch what I refuse. Watch. Just watch. Watch this refuse. Here it is. Here it is here. Here it is right here. Here it is right here in my hand right here. Here it is right here in my right hand right here. I paid for it. I did. I really did. Really I did. I really did pay for it. I paid for it really. I really paid. Money was involved. Money was an issue. Money was exchanged. Do you want to know how long it took? I never said how long it took. How long could it have taken? How could it have taken so long? How could it have taken so long to say what I said I saw? I got it. I got it every day. Every day I got what I got. I got what I could get. Get it? I got it. I got what I got. I get what I got. I get it. I got to get it. Every day I got to get it. Every day I get. I get every day. What can I do? I do what I can. I do what I can do. I can do what I can do. What I do I can do. I can do what? What? Tell me. You tell me. You tell me what I can do. You can tell me what I can do. I shouldn't have had the second one. I should never have had the second one. I never should have had the second one. I should have never had the second one. Never should I have had the second one. I should have had the second one never. I should write a number somewhere. I should write a number somewhere on all this stuff. Somewhere I should maybe write a number on all this stuff. I should number all this stuff. I should stuff a number somewhere on all this stuff. I should stuff a number somewhere. I should stuff all this stuff somewhere. It's tough. This stuff is tough to stuff. This stuff is stuff to stuff. Could it happen? Is it conceivable? It could happen. It is conceivable. Isn't it conceivable? Isn't it conceivable it could happen? Could it be conceivable it could happen? Could it happen to be conceivable? Could it be conceived? Could you conceive of it happening? Could you conceive of it conceivably happening? Could you happen to conceive of it conceivably happening? Could you conceive? Remember what I said before? Remember what I said before I said what I said? Remember? I said, 'Remember.' Before I said what I said what I said was, 'Remember.' Remember? She's gone. She won't be back. I checked. I thought I should check. I should check, I thought. Should I check, I thought. Should I check my thought? There was one. There was another one. There was another nother one. Another other nother. One other. Any other.

How many others were there? Were there any others? Were the others any others? Were there many others? Were the others many? Were the others many others? There was always another. You know that, right? I don't have to tell you there was always another. There always was another. There was always another one. Not always one. Never not another one. That was not another, was it? Was it another? There was one other. There was only one other. There was always only one other. I keep thinking she might come back. She might keep coming back, I keep thinking. She might keep thinking back. Keep thinking back. Keep thinking. 'Keep thinking,' they say. They say, 'Keep thinking.' Say I keep thinking. Say, 'Keep thinking.' Say it. Say it now. 'Keep thinking.' I keep thinking. I keep thinking I should say. I got nothing done today. I got no thing done today. Not one no thing. No thing not one. Not no thing one. I said I would. Didn't I say I would? Wouldn't I say I did? Didn't I do what I said I would? Don't I do what I say I'll do? I'll do what I say I'll do. Did I say I wouldn't? Wouldn't I say I did? I'll say I did. I did all I said. I'll say all I said I did. I'll say all I did. All I did was say. She pretended she knew. She knew she pretended. I didn't pretend. I don't pretend. I don't pretend to know. I don't pretend to know what I'm not. I don't know what to pretend I'm not. I don't know to pretend. I don't know what I'm not to pretend. What am I thinking? Am I thinking? Was I thinking? I was thinking. I remember thinking. I remember thinking everything. I remember everything I was thinking. I remember thinking I was everything. I wouldn't say 'worried.' I would use another word. What word would I use? I don't know. I don't know what word I would use. I don't want to worry about what word I would use for 'worried.' I'm not worried about what word I would use for 'worried.' Would you have me worry about what word I would use for 'worried'? Would you have me worry? Would you worry? Would you worry that I don't worry about what word I would use for 'worried'? I would use another word. I don't know what other word. Do you worry I would use a word that I don't know for 'worried'? Should I worry that you worry? Should I worry at all? What should I worry about? Should I worry about you? Are you worried about me? I'm not worried about me. Why should you be worried about me? Why should I worry that you might be worried? I'm not going to leave. I can see no reason to leave. There is no reason to leave. There is no reason I can see to leave. I can see there might be reason to leave. It seems reasonable to believe there might be reason to leave. I believe that to leave might be reasonable. I believe to leave. I leave to believe. I am not leaving. I am believing. I am believing in not ever leaving. Believe me. Don't leave me. I should do more. The more I should do the less I do. The less I do the more I should do. I do more. I do do more. Sometimes I do. Sometimes I do and sometimes I should do. Sometimes I think I do do what I should. Sometimes I think I do what I should do. Sometimes what I do I do think I should. Sometimes what I think I should do I do. I should do what I do think sometimes. Sometimes I do. Sometimes I do do what I think I should. Yesterday we spoke. Yesterday we didn't speak. It wasn't yesterday we spoke. We spoke the day before yesterday. The day before we didn't speak we spoke. The day before we spoke we spoke. We spoke the day before we spoke. She told me I could stay. I could stay, she told me. 'Stay,' she told me. 'Stay.' She told me to stay. I didn't want to stay. I told her I would stay. I didn't want to leave. I said I had to go. Every day I am astounded. She is going to come and stay with me. She is going to come and she is going to stay with me. I could do it still. I could still do it. Still I could do it. I'm allowed. If I want. I'm allowed if I want. If I want I'm allowed. I decided to lie down. I decided I needed to lie down. I lay down.

I got up. I decided to get up. I decided I needed to get up. I stayed up. I waited. I stayed up and I waited. It was late. I was up. I was waiting up. I could do it now. There is no excuse. The things I did. It was days. It was nights. I spent days. I spent nights. I don't know why. I didn't want to. I didn't need to. I didn't need. I didn't. I did. The days were going to end. The days were going to have to end. There were days that didn't end. There were days that wouldn't end. Days and days that wouldn't end. Days and nights that didn't end. Fucking long days. Fucking long nights. I wanted to watch. I wanted her to watch. I said nothing. Do you understand? I said not a thing. Do you understand what I am saying? Not one single fucking thing. I keep her with me here. Do you want to look? Do you want to see? I keep her here. So much is disappearing. So much has disappeared. I keep her here with me. I want to stop. Waste of time the time I waste. I am almost there. I am so close. I will soon be there. Soon I will be there. Soon I will be gone. I should have stayed away. Should I have stayed away? I wasn't thinking. I wasn't thinking clearly. Clearly I wasn't thinking. It is over now. Whatever it was. Whatever it was it is over. It was whatever it was and now it is not. Whatever it was when it was it is now not. You get it. You get over it. Whatever it is you get, you get over it. Over and over you get what you get and over and over you get over what you get. You get what you get over and you get over what you get. It is nothing. Nothing is what it is. It is what it is and nothing is what it is. It is nothing now. What it is is nothing now. Nothing is now. Now is nothing. There will be no more. There will be not any more. No more will there be not. Not no more. No more not. There will not any be more. She came with me. She came with me sometimes. I don't feel the way. I thought I would. The way I feel I don't. Feel the way I thought I would. The way I feel I thought I would. Not the way I would I thought. I should feel the way I should. There will be more. There will always be more. There always will be more. There will always be more always. There should be more everywhere. There should always be more everywhere. Everywhere there should be more. I've said it before. I'll say it again. It was right here. I had it right here. Here it was. Right here. I had it. I get up. I get up, go out. Go out, come back. Come back, sit down. Sit down, get up. Get up, go out. Go out, come back. I cannot move. I cannot bring myself to move. I try not to think about it. I think about what I try not to think about. I try not to think about what I think about. I try not to think about what I try not to think about that I think about. I think about what I try not to think about. I try not to think about what I try not to think about that I think about that I try not to think about. I try not to think. I am less interested. I am interested less. There is less that interests me. That that interests me interests me less. I am less interested in that that interests me. In that I am interested. In that I am more interested. Every day the same. The same thing every day. Always every day. The same thing always every day. As well as always every night. I told her to leave. I asked her to leave. I wanted her to leave. I needed her to leave. There was no difference. What was the difference? There was no difference. I should do something. I should do more. I should do something more. I should be doing something more. More than I am doing. I should be doing more. More of something. I should be something more. This place is mine. It is my place. Here we are again. At this place here again we are. Again, once more, this place, we are. Here again we are this place. At this one place again once more. This place again we are at this. This place again once more we are. I should be exercising more. I should be exercising. I should be. I should. I. This is something I will do again. I am adding nothing. I'm not adding nothing. I know what she is. I know who she says. They are never going to see me again. They are never going to know who I am. They are going to see me once. They are going to see me only once. I am not going back. I am going once. I am going only once. I am not returning. I am once. I am only once. I will be a part. I will take a part. Take a part, be a part. Take apart. Be apart. I try to forget. Some days I try to forget. Some days I do not try to forget. I try to forget every day. Come on. Hurry up. There's no rush. I am not well. I am not feeling well. I am not feeling well at all. I should not have said. I never should have said. Now I see. I am not well at all feeling. Now I can see. I can see now. I am well at not feeling. I cannot feel well. I cannot feel. I can now see. See? Now I can. I am not feeling. I am not at all. Do you know what word I like? 'Don't talk like that,' I said. 'Please don't talk like that,' I said. 'I don't want to hear you talk like that,' I said. Suck. Hung up. I don't know if they are comfortable. I don't know if they feel comfortable. Sitting down, they feel comfortable. Standing up, they feel comfortable. They did a good job. They did a pretty good job. Keep counting. Don't stop. It's not what you think. It's not who you think. What do you think? Who do you think? I tried to forget. The decision was me. The decision I made. I made the decision.

I tried not to think. The decision was made. Why not finish telling you? I am almost finished telling you. I could finish telling you. I could finish telling you what I am almost finished telling you until I finished telling you. Never not stop telling you. Never not stop finishing. She handed me a razor. Told me to shave. I do it myself. I do it all myself. Whatever there is. All that there is. I do it myself. You don't believe me. Cook. Clean. Wash. Dry. That doesn't mean it isn't true. 'Shave,' she said. Boil. Crack. Peel. Pickle. The notice came. I know you don't believe me. I saw her. She was there. I shaved. I could see her. I have the notice here. The notice came today. There she was. I wanted something. I wanted to have something. I wanted to have something ready. She was there. I wanted something ready. I wanted something to be ready. I wanted to have something to be ready. I will again. No doubt again. I will no doubt. No doubt I will. Again no doubt. Again I will. Against my will? My will no doubt. No doubt my will. I doubt my will. Again I doubt. My doubt no doubt. Again. At last. At last, again. Again, at last. Who knows? Not me. I set the alarm. I got into bed. Pulled up the covers. Turned off the light. Turned onto my side. I waited. I thought. You want to know something? You want to know something else? This is what I have. This is all I have. I have all of this. All of this is what I have. All of what I have is this.

Acknowledgements

Thank you: Derek McCormack, Hal Niedzviecki, Ken Sparling and Alana Wilcox.

About the Author

GEOFFREY BROWN is the author of *Notice* (Gutter Press, 1999). In 2003, 'Listen,' an excerpt from *Self-Titled* originally published in *Broken Pencil*, was shortlisted for the Journey Prize. Brown is also a photographer.

Typeset in Dante and printed and bound at the Coach
House on bpNichol Lane, 2004.

Edited by Derek McCormack
Seen through the press by Alana Wilcox
Cover photograph by Geoffrey Brown
Cover design by Rick/Simon

Coach House Books
401 Huron Street (rear) on bpNichol Lane
Toronto, Ontario
M5S 2G5

1 800 367 6360
416 979 2217

mail@chbooks.com
www.chbooks.com